W9-CAI-863

MADAME CLAUDE
Le Pistoulet
Route de l'Esprit de Verité
Jegun dans le Gers,
France

The Circle of Kindness

An Irish Journey of the Heart

Jana Kolpen & Mary Tiegreen

Stewart, Tabori & Chang
New York

Beyond the bluest ocean and over the green hills, along the winding road that passes the murmuring sheep and the skylark that sings in the giant oak tree, through a small crooked gate and down the narrow path lies a small pink cottage overlooking the sea. In all of Ireland there isn't a finer place to have a cup of tea and witness the wonders of life that are offered to us every day.

A rosebush heavy with fragrant pink blossoms arches over the doorway, and the thatch roof protects all within from sun and rain. And inside the kitchen a young woman with fiery red hair often sings to her cat as she bakes wonderful, warm loaves of Irish bread.

It was to this enchanted spot that Mademoiselle J. had been invited to spend a time of quiet repose.

She arrived on a beautiful afternoon and was greeted
at the crooked gate by a committee of fat hens and a
sweet-faced cow with the kindest eyes in all the world.
The red-haired woman waved from the doorway. Her warm
smile made Mademoiselle feel as if she were coming home.

Herding the committee back toward the henhouse, the woman
with the fiery red hair introduced herself and her cackling friends. Finola was
the fat one; Mairead the best looking; Una and Margaret were sisters; Colleen,
Kelly, and Kate liked to dance; and McGillicuddy was named after a fellow in
the village who wore a floppy red hat and bore a striking resemblance to this
particular chicken. And the woman herself was called Shannon.

Mademoiselle was overcome by
Shannon's joyfulness. In fact,
the redhead was the most joyful
person Mademoiselle had ever
met. She felt lifted and light.

That evening they sat at the
ancient oak table in the cozy
kitchen. All was quiet outside
and the committee settled into
their own home, making eggs
for the morning breakfast.
Shannon poured Mademoiselle
a large pint of dark, thick ale, and
they laughed and talked of many things,
speaking with reverence and affection about their wonderful friend Madame
Claude, who resided at the magical French farmhouse known as Pistoulet.

Weary from her journey, Mademoiselle bid Shannon good night and
climbed the narrow staircase to her room, which overlooked the sea. An
enormous bed piled with feather pillows invited her to climb in and have a
rest. Mademoiselle laid her head on the soft downy pillows and drifted into
a deep sleep. Outside her window, the sea sang its rhythmic lullaby.

Shannon's kitchen was a place of
wonderment and heart.

The cool morning light filtered through the lace
curtains as Rory the ruffled rooster sang to the arrival
of the dawn. Mademoiselle awoke from her dream,
amidst feather pillows in her cozy room, to the deeply
comforting aroma of baking bread.

As Mademoiselle descended the narrow staircase, the baking bread infused
the morning with the comfort and coziness of her childhood. (Her passion
for bread ran deep. She had been known to forgo fine delicacies for a
simple slice of warm, freshly baked bread.) Shannon greeted her with a
smile and a large cup of tea. Mademoiselle's eyes and appetite grew as
she watched Shannon prepare a hearty Irish breakfast.

"Perhaps today you'd like to learn the secrets of the perfect Irish soda
bread!" Mademoiselle, who loved cooking and often thought she could
live in a kitchen forever, was thrilled with the opportunity. "First we must
go into town to pick up a little of this and that."
From the old shed beside the henhouse
Shannon emerged with a bicycle built for
two, and off they went.

Beyond the crooked gate, they followed the winding road past the murmuring sheep and the giant oak tree. At a crossroads they turned right and descended a hill that entered a deep green forest.

Towering yew trees, older than time, arched across the road with a tangle of branches that turned day into night. Mademoiselle suddenly felt as if she'd entered another world. They rolled alongside a babbling brook and crossed a singing bridge that carried them over a sparkling stream.

The ancient forest opened onto a lush green meadow dotted with cows that were a curious shade of blue. Beyond this meadow was an elegant Irish country house set far back from the road.

Mademoiselle stopped and took in a deep, deep breath and felt lighthearted and enchanted by this very funny place.

On they rolled into the village of Dunwalsh-by-the-Sea, a town of modest demeanor. Rolling by a quiet inn, they passed a rather parsimonious, painfully perfect garden, a few small, ordinary shops, and a very peculiar thatched roof cottage with a sign that read Just Plain Haircuts.

O'Connell Street

Riding along O'Connell Street they nearly ran over a group of Twelve Exuberant English Revelers who had stopped to sing "Happy Birthday" to their friend George, right in the middle of the road.

Mr. & Mrs. E. E. Entwhistle and Miss Plumbush often enjoy harmonizing well into the evening.

At the place where Old Meadow Lane meets Doolin Street, Shannon waved to Mr. McGillicuddy, a round man with a red hat that flopped to one side, and stopped to help a lost soul with a tattered map find his way.

Arriving at the market, Shannon selected a large wheel of cheese from Mr. Cashel Blue and two heavy bags of brown wheat flour from the extremely tall farmer who lived down the road. Balanced on the bicycle, she and Mademoiselle made the trek home.

*It has been scientifically proven that Irish blue cows
produce the most sumptuous of cheeses.*

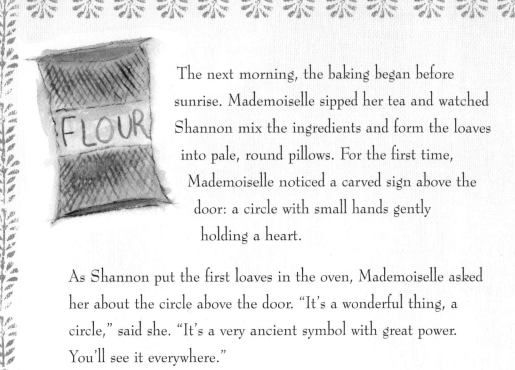

The next morning, the baking began before
sunrise. Mademoiselle sipped her tea and watched
Shannon mix the ingredients and form the loaves
into pale, round pillows. For the first time,
Mademoiselle noticed a carved sign above the
door: a circle with small hands gently
holding a heart.

As Shannon put the first loaves in the oven, Mademoiselle asked
her about the circle above the door. "It's a wonderful thing, a
circle," said she. "It's a very ancient symbol with great power.
You'll see it everywhere."

"The circle has no beginning and no end. In our lives we
may travel far from home, but we will
someday come back to where we began."
With that, the sweet-faced cow
stuck her head in the window.

Heartwarming Recipes from the Pink Cottage

Brown Bread & Irish Soda Bread

May you always have warm bread
on a cold morning.

During her travels far from home, Mademoiselle had spent much time exploring her own heart and in turn the heart of the world. Through her experiences she had come to understand the power we hold in our hands and in our hearts.

She now began to understand why Madame Claude had suggested she visit Merriweather Cottage. It was here in this land of many greens that Mademoiselle J. would find the generosity of spirit and compassion that turns the world.

There was a warmth and wonder that filled the simple kitchen. As the aroma of bread filled the room, Mademoiselle saw a line of people forming outside the cottage door. Shannon explained that they come twice a week from as far away as Dingle to buy her famous breads. Mademoiselle J. watched as the people dropped a few coins in a ceramic pot on the table for each round, wonderful loaf.

Even the smallest kindness can change the world.

There isn't a finer place in the world to witness the wonders of life
that are offered to us every day.

The breads of Merriweather Cottage are much sought after and talked about. Each warm, fresh-baked loaf nourishes the soul and brightens a lackluster life.

Occasionally a poor soul arrived looking forlorn and humble, having perhaps experienced a difficult struggle with life. Shannon would greet them warmly and discreetly slip a fat loaf of bread and a wedge of blue cheese into their basket, free of charge.

At certain points, Mademoiselle would notice her reach into a colorful wooden box that sat at the edge of the table. Inside were dozens of small, bright objects. "A blessing for the journey," she would say, and would whisper something that would make them smile as she discretely handed them the small charm.

"My grandmother always told us that a little bit of kindness can change the world," she would say with a wink and a warm smile.

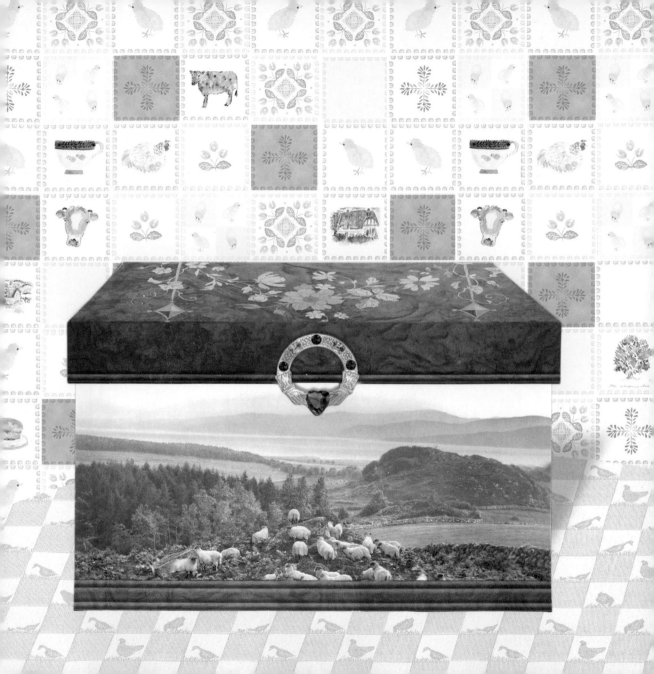

One morning Mademoiselle found Shannon in the kitchen preparing a basket of Heartwarming Brown Bread, fresh raisin scones, and a fat, round jar of homemade strawberry jam. "I was thinking it might be a nice thing to bring some goodness to a friend down the road." Her green eyes twinkled as she spoke. "She's a dear thing, but always alone. Sometimes I bring her a basket of warmth, and share a cup of kindness with her to help her pass the time."

According to Shannon, the Lady was once a beautiful and vibrant woman. Her joy for living was legendary. But with the passing of her husband several years ago, she seemed to retreat into herself. Her children had moved away and she lost interest in most things.

In her youth, the Legendary Lady attended many lavish parties in London, Paris, and Dublin. She was known for her beauty and sweet demeanor.

"She's always glad for a little company now and then." Mademoiselle J. offered to deliver the basket to the Legendary Lady. Shannon smiled as she opened the wooden box and handed Mademoiselle one of the small, bright charms. "You'll be needing one of these," she said. Mademoiselle held it tight in her hand, afraid to let go. It seemed to radiate a comforting warmth.

Heartwarming Recipes
from the Pink Cottage

Time-Passing Scones
& Giving Hearts

Giving Hearts
These sweet heart cookies help
promote the giving spirit.

Mix two cups of the sweetest sugar with ½ cup of the freshest golden butter from a cow with the kindest eyes in all the world owned by a tender-hearted local farmer. Acquire two large eggs laid that morning at sunrise. Beat them into the mixture. Add 2½ cups of flour that has many purposes, 2 teaspoons of potent baking powder and 1 teaspoon of only the purest vanilla extracted from a gently picked vanilla bean.

Beat the ingredients together in a significant bowl received as gift from a loving soul. Form the dough into a ball, flatten, and wrap in plastic. Chill for 3 to 4 hours.

Sprinkle a well-worn board with flour. Roll out the dough. First cut out dough with a 2" ruffled round cookie cutter. Then gently press each one with a heart-shaped cutter repeating the words "A kind heart is a giving heart." Bake on a cookie sheet for 7-12 minutes at 375 degrees. When cool serve as is or decorate with cookie icing.

Always remember: The best gifts
come from the heart.

There is always time
for friendship.

Nestled in the rolling green fields was the grand country house of the Legendary Lady of Shanagarry. The stately home with many rooms was surrounded by endless gardens and towering trees. A curious white peacock patrolled the grounds, occasionally displaying the delicate splendor of its tail. As Mademoiselle approached the house she noticed a tall, whimsical man sporting a long gray ponytail, who was busy in the front garden pouring birdseed on the lawn in the shape of large letters of the alphabet. "I'm teaching the birds to read," he explained. "I've already taught them to count!"

Mademoiselle J. approached the door and knocked timidly. Slowly the giant door opened to reveal a very small, elegant woman with silver hair and bright gray eyes. "Come in!" she said, and her smile lit up the dark entryway.

"I have some bread and scones for you from—"

"Yes, I see! Isn't she wonderful? She never forgets!" The Legendary Lady seemed delighted to have company.

Mademoiselle found herself being escorted to a lovely sunroom where fragrant jasmine and honeysuckle vines grew up through the floor and graced the walls with pungent flowers. Beyond the doorway she could see a palatial ballroom decorated in tapestries and rich brocade curtains, and beyond that, an enormous dining hall.

It had been some time since the Lady had hosted one of her celebrated feasts. In her joyful youth, her guests would travel from far and farther in order to attend her grand buffets. She would often house one hundred guests at a time in the splendor of her grand manor house, covered in ivy. They would stay for days on end, enjoying only the finest at a magnificent buffet feast, listening to the best musicians in all of Ireland, walking through the exquisite gardens, and sleeping soundly in palatial rooms.

But now her children had departed to live their own lives far away, and with the passing of her husband, life had lost its

luster. For many years she had resided alone in the grand country estate with only her servants to provide occasional company. She had grown accustomed to her life, but she missed the laughter and joy that friendship brings.

The Lady opened a tall cabinet that was filled top to bottom with dishes, serving bowls, and crystal wine goblets. Mademoiselle J. had never seen so many dishes in all her life! There must have been at least two hundred plates and just as many teacups.

The Legendary Lady was known throughout Ireland as being the perfect hostess.

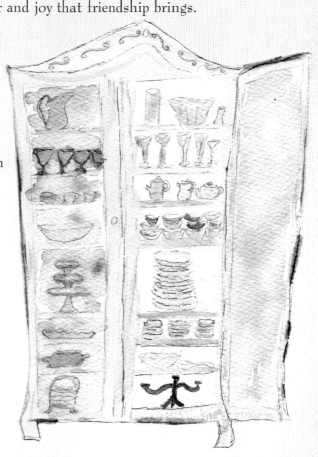

The Legendary Lady carefully removed two fine china cups and saucers and placed them on a tray. They settled in the garden room with a generous pot of jasmine tea. There was something about Mademoiselle J. that felt comforting and familiar to the Legendary Lady.

They spoke of many things that sunny afternoon in the glorious garden room, enjoying cups of aromatic jasmine tea and the delicious Time-Passing Scones. The Legendary Lady shared memories of many a grand party and the friends who would dance and laugh and toast their futures. Now all seemed quiet and her sweet face became once again wistful. Suddenly Mademoiselle remembered the charm. "I'd almost forgotten," she said, "but this is for you." She handed the bright circle to the Lady, who seemed quite dazzled by its brilliance and powerful warmth.

TREASURED MEMORIES

FORGET ME NOT

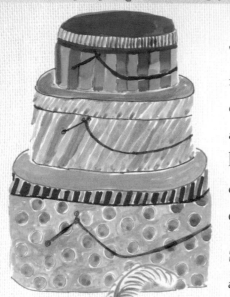

The Legendary Lady rose from her chair and exclaimed, "On such a day as this, one should take in a bit of fresh country air!" She opened a closet by the large front door. Inside the closet were stacks of hatboxes.

She handed Mademoiselle a most exquisite purple automobile bonnet with elegant plumes and a long chiffon scarf to tie under the chin. The Legendary Lady selected a discreet green velvet chapeau.

The Tall Gentleman was waiting outside the door with the Bentley, and off they went! The Legendary Lady, who seemed so frail when they first met at the door, seemed more vigorous now as they rolled down the road.

Laughing lightly, she pointed out this and that shop and shared stories of Dunwalsh's most interesting citizens, all the while waving to old friends along the way.

As they passed a shop called Fitzpatrick and Son, Ltd.: Makers of Fine Furniture, Mademoiselle J. saw a young man sitting in the window, looking forlorn. On the door was a sign that said Going Out of Business.

The Legendary Lady seemed quite shocked at the idea that this shop would be closing its doors. She paused for a moment and then reached in her purse and began scribbling a note on a small piece of paper.

A smile brightened her face as she announced that she had the intention of commissioning a table. A very, very long table that would accommodate at least thirty-six guests at the same time! Mademoiselle was quite taken aback by the Legendary Lady's request, since it was clear that she most often dined alone and already had many tables, both large and small, in her elegant home.

The Legendary Lady
Singingbridge Road
Shanagarry,
Ireland

Folding the note, she slipped the charm into the middle and tucked it into Mademoiselle's pocket, saying, "Darling girl, would you be so kind as to bring this order for one very, very long dining table to the lad tomorrow morning?" Mademoiselle agreed that she would be delighted.

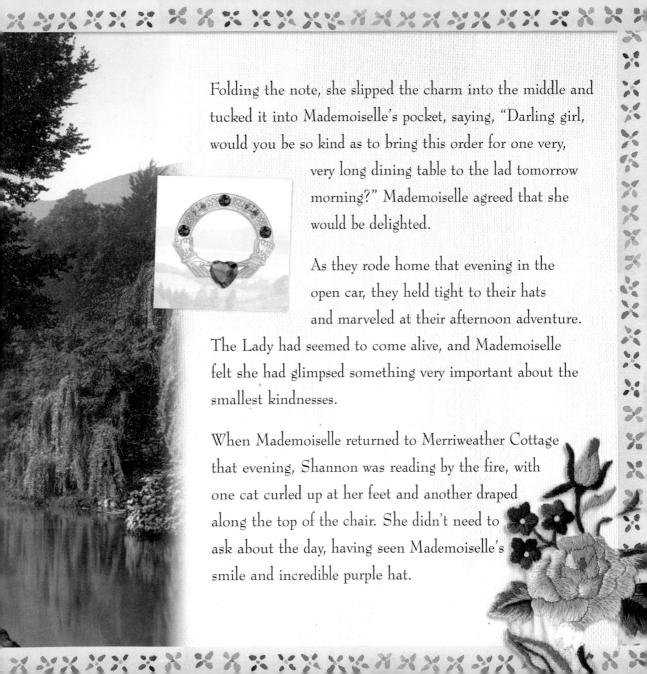

As they rode home that evening in the open car, they held tight to their hats and marveled at their afternoon adventure. The Lady had seemed to come alive, and Mademoiselle felt she had glimpsed something very important about the smallest kindnesses.

When Mademoiselle returned to Merriweather Cottage that evening, Shannon was reading by the fire, with one cat curled up at her feet and another draped along the top of the chair. She didn't need to ask about the day, having seen Mademoiselle's smile and incredible purple hat.

The next morning, over steaming mugs of tea, Mademoiselle told Shannon about her day with the Legendary Lady. "She's asked me to bring this note to a gentleman in the village. A man who makes furniture." Shannon smiled. "I heard he'd be needing some work." Mademoiselle couldn't contain her curiosity about the young man. "He's a fine craftsman and a special man. The son of a fine cabinet maker. He has as much respect for trees as he has for you and me," said Shannon, and went on to tell Mademoiselle about him.

Fitzpatrick grew up in the Whispering Forest and learned the secrets of the wood. As a young lad he was fond of walking alone in the ancient forest where the tree spirits reside. He spent his days listening to the music of life—the wind that bothered the leaves in the highest branches of the tallest trees, a choir of birds singing at dawn, the echoing song of a single bird after the rain, a rustle of autumn leaves as a fox scurries home, the springtime chorus of frogs, the silent softness of snow falling through bare branches. So gifted was he that they say he could even hear the voices of the trees themselves. Fitzpatrick had a profound connection to the earth and a reverence for life.

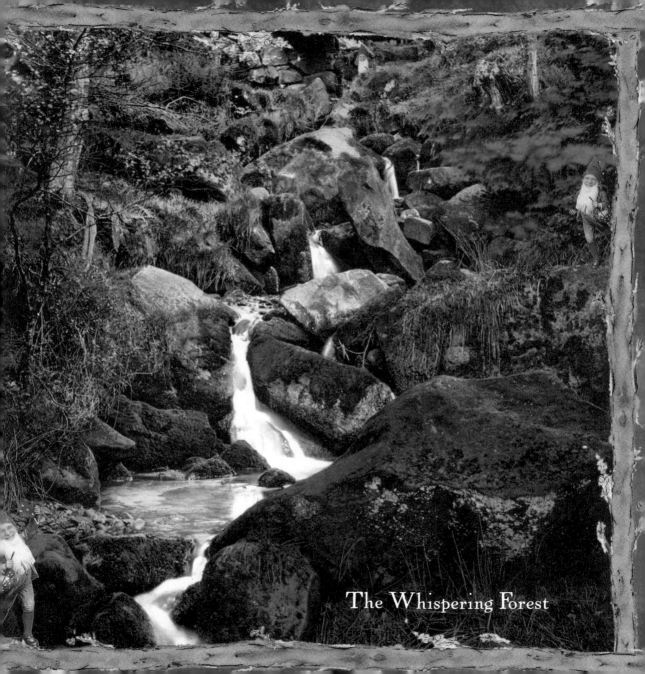

The Whispering Forest

"He makes very special furniture for people who need the power of the trees to help them in their lives."

Mademoiselle appeared perplexed.

"His furniture is different, you see. Some would call it magic, but it's simply filled with spirit. A while ago, a young couple came to him in need of a bed. They had been married for some time but had yet to be blessed with a child. He built them a wonderful Bed of Becoming, made of graceful birch, 'the Lady of the Woods.'"

A Bench of Young Branches for one whose life has become rigid and stale, and who needs some flexibility.

Shannon smiled. "It's a tree that possesses the power of beginnings, the seeds of potential. And don't you know, today they have a lovely little girl with a smile more beautiful than a sunrise!"

A Musical Chair

"But lately, a sadness has come over him. You see, no one believes in the wood spirits anymore, and he's taken it very hard. He's not been to the ancient forest for many months. It's like he's lost a friend. And I'm afraid he can't afford to continue as he is."

A profound reverence for trees lies deep in the hearts of the people of Dunwalsh. Each tree has its own majesty and special powers. For the Bed of Becoming, Fitzpatrick selected the elegant and graceful birch tree, the tree of beginnings and the birth of new life.

Mademoiselle
realized the
importance of bringing
the letter from the Legendary
Lady, and was anxious to meet the
gifted young man.

In the old shed she found the rusty
red bicycle built for one, and with the note tucked
securely in her pocket, off she went. As she passed the giant
oak tree, the skylark sang its sweet song of summer and the
wind whispered through its leaves.

Approaching the
ancient forest, Mademoiselle
wondered what spirits lived in the
wood. It seemed that every tree had a
face that smiled upon her as she passed. She
paused in the cool of the forest and listened for
voices, but heard none.

On she rolled, past the field of curious blue cows.
She saw the Legendary Lady, who was gathering a bouquet
of the brightest pink flowers. She waved a sunny greeting. How
she had changed in just a day! She was still wearing the lovely
green hat, and a rosy color had returned to her cheeks.

As Mademoiselle approached the shop, she saw Fitzpatrick standing in the doorway. He greeted her with a brave smile, and yet he seemed forlorn.

Inside, the workshop was warm and had the smell of freshly cut timber, and sawdust covered the tables and benches like a blanket of soft snow. Mademoiselle fumbled in her many pockets and finally retrieved the folded note, handing it to the young man.

As he opened the note, one could see a considerable amount of money tucked inside. The bright charm was there as well, and it illuminated his handsome face with the glow of a warm fire. As Fitzpatrick read the letter, his eyes widened and a smile returned to his face. "A table!" he exclaimed. "I shall make her the finest table in all of Ireland! And will she be needing chairs?"

"I don't really know," said Mademoiselle, a bit flustered, "but I think she did mention something about thirty-six people…"

This once quiet man would not stop talking! So thrilled was the gifted craftsman with his newfound project that he invited Mademoiselle to dine with him immediately at a charming inn across the road. Mademoiselle was perplexed, as it was only 10:00 AM, but the gifted craftsman explained that this particular restaurant was only open between normal mealtimes and that the menu was rather unusual.

The owner, it seems, was a bit of an upside-down man. Everything in his life was outside the norm, which made him a most charming and whimsical host.

The Inn Between had no address. If one wanted to find it, one had to look in between the barbershop and the bakery. Its sign proclaimed that it was "open in between breakfast, lunch, and dinner Wednesdays, Saturdays, and every other Tuesday."

The Inn Between

MENU

It is wise to enjoy the
inn between moments of life.

Mademoiselle found the menu quite amusing, and selected the Tipsy Mushrooms on Toast. It was an enjoyable thing to dine in between, for no particular reason at all. Fitzpatrick was fine company indeed and seemed so excited about his work!

Just then, the innkeeper appeared in the doorway with a bright smile and a tray of Dingle Toasties that he passed around to all the grateful guests. Mademoiselle felt happy just being in the presence of this funny man.

The whimsical innkeeper introduced himself as Himself, and plopped himself down at the table, in between Mademoiselle and Fitzpatrick.

Mademoiselle noticed two very glum young women slouched in a booth sipping cold coffee and staring into space. She asked Himself about them.

Tipsy Mushrooms on Toast

Gather 2 pounds of the wildest mushrooms. Sauté them on medium heat in 2 tablespoons of oil for about 10 minutes until they shed tears of laughter. Add a tablespoon of sweet butter made from the milk of a tipsy cow and stir occasionally for about 8 minutes, or until mushrooms darken.

Add 1 medium shallot, minced, and 2 sprigs of wild thyme from the meadow of a happy farmer and cook until soft. Season with salt and pepper. Add 2 to 3 tablespoons of Marsala and cook until the liquid has evaporated. Get really daring and substitute Bailey's Irish Cream!

Serve on hearty brown bread toasts and be prepared for wobbly dinner guests.

They were sisters, he explained, and both had lost the passion for life. Molly, the girl with the peculiar coiffure, was a hairdresser.

The home of the Bored Hairdresser was predictably ragged.

It seemed that ever since she had been a child, Molly had always dreamed of somewhere else. No grass was greener than in her own backyard, but she could only see the weeds. Bored with everything in her world, she often came to work in the morning grumbling, and left at the end of the day without once sharing a smile. And the haircuts she administered on the unsuspecting were nothing short of criminal!

LADIES HAIR CUTS

A
B
C
D — NO LONGER AVAILABLE

MEN'S

A
B

"It's amazing that anyone still goes to her shop," said Himself, "but I think she's a sweet girl underneath it all." Mademoiselle's heart went out to her.

It was never Molly's intention to make her customers leave looking like mushrooms.

It seemed that her sister Dolly was much the same. A once-talented weaver, she used to make warm, colorful shawls and sweaters from the soft wool she gathered from her very own sheep. Her sweaters wrapped you in comfort while her scarves made you feel warm and protected.

Ever since she was a small lamb, Delilah had displayed a flirtatious nature.

One unfortunate day, her favorite sheep, Delilah, fell in love with a ram from the other side of the mountain and off she wandered, never to be seen again. Dolly was beside herself and never recovered her joy. The loss took all the color from her life, and she began weaving the most dreadfully dull, uncomfortable sweaters and scarves made from wool of a nameless color. Mademoiselle could imagine wearing one of her sweaters and began feeling rather itchy and twitchy!

"The sisters have lost their sense of wonder," said Himself, and he sighed.

With his renewed enthusiasm for life, Fitzpatrick had an idea. As it was a warm summer day, he pondered aloud, wouldn't it be a fine thing to do to invite the girls on a picnic? Both Mademoiselle and Himself heartily agreed.

Himself enlisted Mademoiselle's help in the kitchen preparing a venerable repast, while Fitzpatrick invited the girls on the adventure. They were reluctant at first, but were ultimately charmed by Fitzpatrick.

Into the oversize basket went a shepherd's pie, a just-picked green-leaf salad dotted with the colorful flowers of summer, a loaf of Heartwarming Brown Bread from Shannon's pink cottage, four lemon shandies, and a mouthwatering double coffee cake with a rich coffee buttercream frosting, an intense coffee glaze, and coffee-soaked walnuts.

As they drove along, Molly grumbled and Dolly stared out the window drearily. And along they rolled, past the rich green fields and murmuring sheep until they reached the top of a hill. Before them was the most beautiful vista Mademoiselle had ever seen.

Not all those who
wander are lost.

The blanket was spread upon the ground under
the shelter of a giant oak tree with an ancient face, and
the group settled into an afternoon of delicious food,
sparkling champagne, wonderful stories, and laughter.

As they toasted their good fortune for having such a fine day,
Fitzpatrick asked for silence. "Listen to the wind," he whispered.
As the wind rushed through the branches of the tree and
down the glen with a sound so soft and sweet,
Dolly could almost imagine the wind was
speaking to her.

A barn swallow flew across the sky in swift loops
and swoops. Fitzpatrick shared with them the marvels
of the bird's journey, coming six thousand miles
from South Africa every spring just to return
to this blessed spot. The Bored and
Colorless Sisters looked up
in awe.

Next Mademoiselle passed around little plates of coffee-walnut cake. Fitzpatrick suggested they close their eyes and really taste the first bite of this incredible dessert. Luckily Mademoiselle was sitting on the ground, for surely she would have fallen off her chair: the flavor was so intense and rich!

From a meadow filled with summer flowers, Fitzpatrick gathered a bouquet of the brightest and most fragrant flowers and gave them to the Colorless Weaver, whose eyes grew wide. Everyone was astonished to see the color returning to the cheeks of the Weaver. She smiled for the first time since Delilah's departure and

Salad of Summer Flowers

Puree 1 cup of wild raspberries picked that day from a hard-to-find patch, ½ cup olive oil, 3 tablespoons white wine vinegar, 1 chopped shallot, and a touch of honey acquired from a local beekeeper. Season with salt and pepper.

Assemble a bowl of the most beautiful baby salad greens. Top with nasturtium flowers and a variety of oranges, raspberries, and other local berries.

Drizzle with the freshly made raspberry vinaigrette, and savor the summer flavors.

announced that she would be weaving pastel scarves
and bright pink sweaters for next fall!

The group of friends turned to Molly. A rainbow had
formed at the edge of the sea, connecting heaven and earth.
At its base was a perfect white pony standing in the
distant meadow. "What a wonderful place," is all she
could say. In Molly's hand, Mademoiselle could see
the bright charm shining in the afternoon sun.

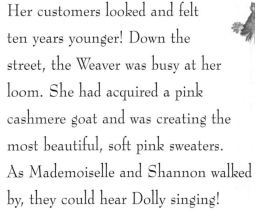

The sisters went back to work with a new joyful attitude.
Even the hairdresser's shop had a light and happy appearance.

Her customers looked and felt
ten years younger! Down the
street, the Weaver was busy at her
loom. She had acquired a pink
cashmere goat and was creating the
most beautiful, soft pink sweaters.
As Mademoiselle and Shannon walked
by, they could hear Dolly singing!

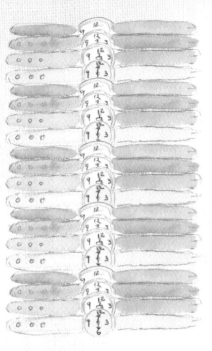

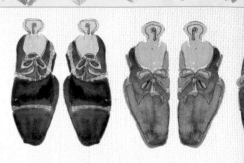

The Perfectionist had a special fondness for the precision of Swiss watches. He checked their accuracy every Wednesday evening at 7:00PM.

Down the street from the Formerly Bored and Colorless Sisters lived their uncle G. Mallone, the Perfectionist. Mallone was a man who believed that everything in life could be just a little bit better and set about trying to make it so. True perfection eluded him as he fussed and fretted the day away, but this did not prevent him from trying to achieve it. All the items in his home had to be set at right angles to one another. His spices were alphabetized, his books organized by color, and his underwear was labeled as to the date of purchase.

His antique teacups were delicately balanced.

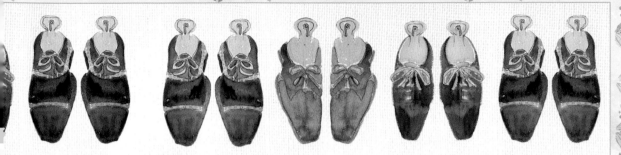

His shoes were polished and organized by date of purchase.

At work he bothered his employees with questions and suggestions as to how to improve their performance from morning till night.

So perfect was he that most people found it difficult to spend time with him. As a result he hadn't many friends. As the years passed, he seemed to grow more meticulous, and the smallest speck of dust would send him into a frenzy. He spent his evenings polishing silver that he never used because he had no friends with whom to dine.

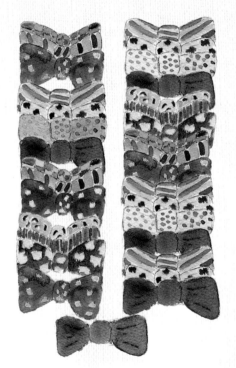

He had a different bow tie for every day of the month.

Mallone's favorite pastime was gardening. He worked tirelessly in his front yard trying to tame the wicked wildness of nature into perfectly formed, sculpted bushes and straight rows of flowers with perfect posture.

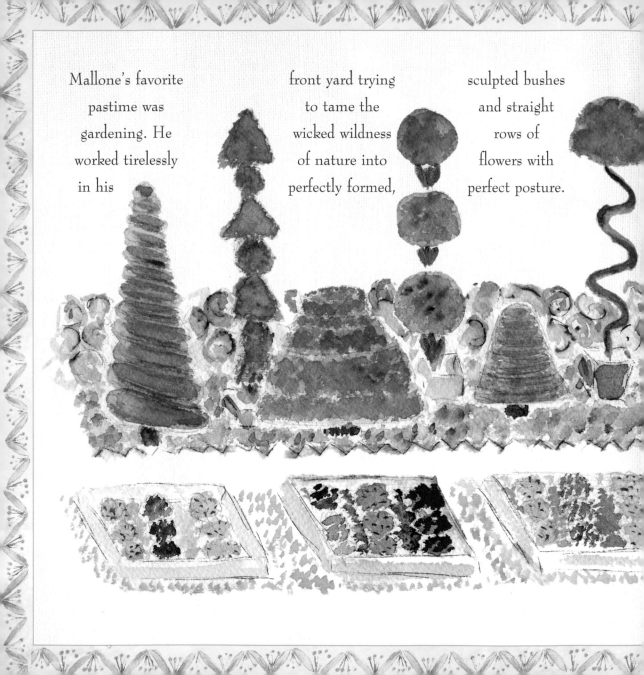

It was on a sunny afternoon that Mademoiselle accompanied the Formerly Bored and Colorless Sisters on a walk about town with their young dog, Ferguson. Less than a year old and full of fun, Ferguson loved to walk, bark, chew, explore, and lick. He was an adorable delight and a bundle of trouble!

As they passed by the Perfectionist's house, the sisters greeted their uncle with cheery smiles, but he was too busy to look up from his garden.

He acknowledged their presence in a punctilious manner and continued to measure and trim a poor hedge into the shape of a perfect cube. His garden is indeed perfect, thought Mademoiselle, but it has no spirit.

Watching Ferguson rolling and tumbling and digging, Molly
had an idea. Back at home, the sisters prepared a basket with
dog food and toys, a leash, and a small note explaining that
the sisters had been called away on a family matter and would
be gone for the weekend. They kindly requested that their
uncle watch over Ferguson until Sunday evening.

Molly and Dolly knew that every Friday afternoon their uncle would take his weekly
constitutional around the village and would pass their window at precisely 4:17 PM
Once past, he would be another forty-seven minutes before returning home.

As they saw him pass the window, they scooted out the back door and ran to his
house. Molly tied Ferguson's leash to the handle of Mallone's perfect front door,
with the note displayed on the top of the basket. On Ferguson's collar,
Molly had attached the bright charm.

Upon returning home at precisely 5:04 PM, Mallone was
taken aback to see a small dog eating his flowers. As he
approached his door, the dog barked and wagged and wet
the pavement in his friendly greeting. Mallone grew faint
at this wild intrusion into his well-constructed world.

He read the note, his mind racing in a panic of possibilities. Try as he might, he could come up with no option but to keep the dog until Sunday evening. He would give the nieces a piece of his mind upon their return.

In the kitchen, Mallone opened the basket while trying to
keep Ferguson from scratching the newly polished floor
and knocking over the carefully arranged furniture. Inside
the basket, he found some very unappetizing food and
a ragged and well-loved stuffed bear, still moist with drool and no
doubt covered with germs. Perhaps a glass of sherry to calm the nerves,
he thought, before his evening repast.

Mallone always had shepherd's pie on Friday nights, and this night would be no
exception. He had locked Ferguson in the cellar where he could do less harm, and
was savoring the aroma of the baking pie when he heard a mournful howl.

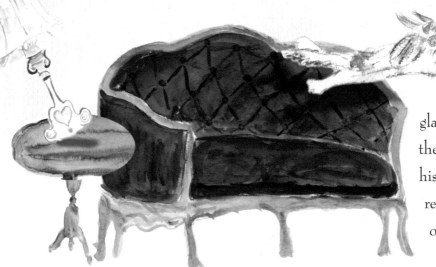

Choosing to ignore
it, Mallone
poured
himself another
glass of sherry to calm
the nerves and sat in
his favorite chair to
read his favorite book
on stain removal.

The mournful howl was now accompanied by a persistent scratching at the door. A door that Mallone had carefully sanded and painted just two weeks before.

It was no use. He could stand it no longer. Mallone rose from his favorite chair and carefully opened the cellar door just a crack to reprimand the dog. A joyful Ferguson knocked him to the floor as he pushed open the door and bounded into the room. Running through the house at breakneck speed, he managed to avoid knocking over most things of value while leaving a trail of dirty paw prints everywhere.

Up the stairs and through the bedroom he ran, disappearing under the bed with one of Mallone's favorite slippers. The sound of slurping and the tearing of fabric under the bed made the poor man wild. Try as he might, he couldn't get Ferguson out from under the bed!

When Mallone was at last successful in shooing the dog out with a handy broom, the chase resumed. Out the door and around the garden and back into the house once more. They raced around the sitting room, where Ferguson managed to circle the room three times without touching the floor, all the while jumping from sofa to chair to end table. Finally Mallone collapsed on the floor in exhaustion and closed his eyes. Life as he knew it was over. He had surrendered at last to the chaos. And yet, he had seemed to survive! An epiphany of sorts filled his brain with a sense of freedom. Freedom from the tyranny of perfection! Mallone began to weep with joy. Sensing that he had perhaps gone too far, Ferguson returned and ever so sweetly began to lick the tears from Mallone's cheeks.

The smell of shepherd's pie burning in the oven brought Mallone back to his senses once more. This was certainly not his typical Friday evening. Things had been turned quite upside down, and the entire house was a tip. Footprints on the sofa, a ruined slipper, a broken lamp, and dinner burned! And yet there was something quite lovable about this dog. Perhaps it was the sherry. He would decide tomorrow.

Mallone went straight to bed that night without eating, having banished Ferguson to a fenced area of the garden. The howling started around 9 PM and by 10:30 PM Ferguson was asleep in Mallone's bed.

On Saturday morning, Mallone worked in his garden with Ferguson by his side, burying bones between the newly planted wildflowers. They dined together in the cozy kitchen on furniture that was no longer at right angles, enjoying their evening meals side by side at the kitchen table. And in the evening when they went to bed, Mallone read Ferguson stories about groundbreaking moments in the history of stain removal. Ferguson's tail would beat a soft rhythm on the bed comforter until he fell asleep and began to snore.

When the nieces returned with Mademoiselle on Sunday evening they found an incredible sight: their uncle and the dog both sitting at the kitchen table sharing a shepherd's pie, and the house a beautiful mess! The light of the charm on Ferguson's collar filled the room with warmth and love.

When Mademoiselle returned to Merriweather Cottage, she couldn't wait to tell Shannon what had transpired. Even Shannon found it hard to believe!

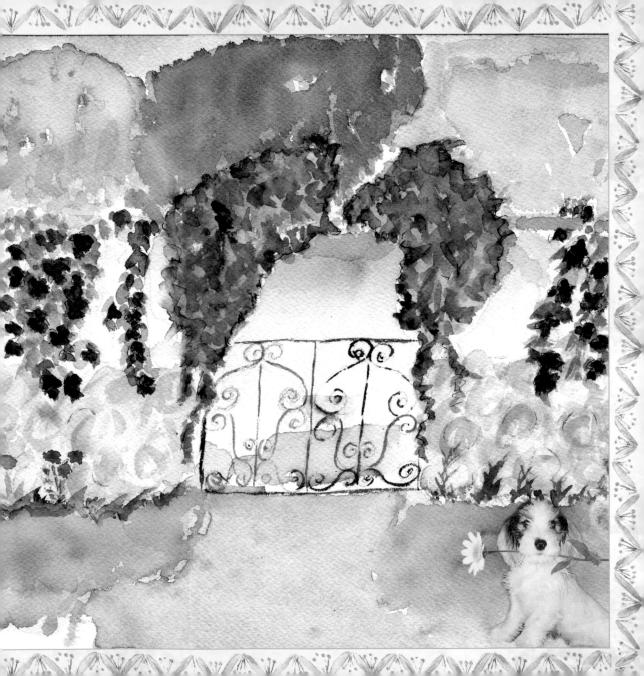

E very day at Merriweather Cottage was a joyful gift, and Mademoiselle felt so much at home. Yet as the bright hues of summer turned into the golden colors of autumn, she began to reflect on her own life and wondered what was to come. Sensing that Mademoiselle needed a bit of fun to fend off a bout of melancholy, Shannon suggested they go into town for an afternoon meal at the Inn Between.

The Inn Between was filled with people in a celebratory mood that day. The Twelve English Revelers had arrived early that morning, and they were all wearing bright sweaters and comforting scarves woven by Delightful Dolly the Colorful Weaver. (And their hairdos had never been more attractive!)

Fitzpatrick was sitting at a table with the Legendary Lady, sketching magical furniture ideas on a paper napkin. Molly and Dolly

A festive Spanish orchestra often entertained at the Inn Between on Friday afternoons.

A BLESSING:
At the old Inn Between,
May the roof be well thatched,
And here at this table
May you both be well matched!

were laughing with friends by the bar, and Himself was doing a little dance in the doorway. There were in fact so many people that there was but one booth left. Shannon motioned for Mademoiselle to have a seat, and that she would be back shortly. Mademoiselle slid into the dark wood booth and felt quite comfortable and cozy. She ordered a pint of dark, thick ale.

On the other side of the dining room stood Mallone with his new companion, Ferguson. He noticed Mademoiselle sitting alone. Somehow she seemed lonely, and at the same time, so lovely. Mallone thought she might need a bit of company.

One hundred years ago, Fitzpatrick's grandfather had constructed the Matchmaking Booth from the wood of the ash, the tree of enchantment, in order to woo his future bride. He carved by hand the delicate borders of ivy, a plant that ensures true love, faithfulness, undying affection, and merrymaking! And finally the table had inlays of hazel in the shape of doves, bestowing wisdom and love on all who sit together in the booth.

Many have met their beloved in the Matchmaking Booth, and it is always a joyous occasion to behold the blossoming of real affection.

The Legendary Lady spared no expense when it came to cheese.

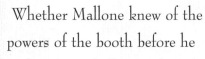

Whether Mallone knew of the powers of the booth before he sat down, we shall never know. But everyone at the Inn Between was witness to the fact that he could not take his eyes off Mademoiselle. Her sweet eyes and small hands bewitched him totally, and she found his laugh to be the most delightful thing she'd ever heard. They smiled and talked and filled the room with joy.

Himself entered the room with a grand gesture and made an announcement. The Legendary Lady had invited one and all to her home to partake in a

The orchestra played on into the wee hours.

feast upon her newly installed Table of Abundance!
A cheer went up and everyone filed out of the door
and down the road to the manor house.

New large Doors of
Welcome, created by
Fitzpatrick, had been
installed to accommodate
the many guests that would be
arriving. Everyone was
in a jovial and
celebratory mood
as the sun set behind the
green hill and the twinkling
stars appeared.

*The fortunate guests
were treated to no less
than seventeen different
types of hors d'oeuvres, including
dippies, toasties, & RagaMuffins.*

Mademoiselle and Mallone were the last to
arrive, with Ferguson by their side. Everyone
shared in their newfound happiness and
wished them well.

As they gathered around the Table of Abundance, Himself proposed the first toast:

"Green be the grass you walk on,
Blue be the skies above you,
Pure be the joys that
surround you,
And true be
the hearts that
love you."

That evening they dined on Irish salmon and drank champagne and toasted their good fortune at the very long table. The Twelve English Revelers sang ballads in twelve-part harmony, and Himself performed an Irish jig. Ferguson feasted on bits of food under the table and, once he was full, found a comfortable overstuffed chair in which to take a snooze.

Out in the garden under the moon, Mademoiselle and Mallone walked hand in hand, savoring the sweetness of the moment. The Matchmaking Booth had worked its magic once again. Mademoiselle felt as if she had known him all her life. Mallone reached in his pocket and pulled out the bright, sparkling circle charm and, holding Mademoiselle's small hand, he placed it as a ring upon her finger.

When they returned to the gathering, everyone was dancing. The Legendary Lady stood and proposed a toast to the happy two.

Through the power of the Doors of Welcome, guests continued to arrive throughout the evening.

A TOAST:

"May you always have

warm words on a cold evening,

A full moon on a dark night,

A soft breeze when summer surrounds you,

A chorus of laughter to lighten the heart,

And the kind smile of a true friend

To welcome you home."

Shannon smiled and raised her glass. As she looked around, she marveled at the changes that had taken place that summer. The Legendary Lady, once lonely and withdrawn, was radiant in a pale pink gown and matching hat. She danced with every man at the party, and displayed her skills as an elegant hostess. Fitzpatrick stood tall and proud, now thriving in his business once again. He and Molly planned another trip to the forest for the following week to witness the beauty of the changing season. Molly looked beautiful with her hair swept up in an elegant do, and was entirely besotted with the handsome carpenter. Dolly—no longer dreary and depressed—dressed in bright colors and glowed with happiness again as she danced with the revelers. Mallone, the former Perfectionist, had become human once more, and embraced his imperfections (as well as Mademoiselle!). And Mademoiselle had never looked happier or more beautiful. Her lightness of heart was captivating!

The circle of kindness was complete.

Mademoiselle J.
Merriweather Cottage
Dunwalsh-by-the-Sea,
Ireland

A Kindness Journal

The smallest kindness can make a big difference. It begins with compassion and listening with your heart. These pages are a place to record your thoughts and acts of kindness. Watch the circle expand as you share your love.
— Mademoiselle J.

"For attractive lips, speak words of kindness."

—Sam Levenson

"No act of kindness, however small, is ever wasted."

—Aesop

"If you want others to be happy, practice compassion. If you want to be happy, practice compassion."

—Dalai Lama

"Blessed is he who speaks a kindness; thrice blessed is he who repeats it."

—Arabian Proverb

"In compassion lies the world's true strength."

—Buddha

"Do your little bit of good where you are; it's those little bits of good put together that overwhelm the world."

—Archbishop Desmond Tutu

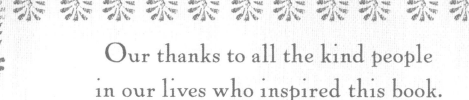

Our thanks to all the kind people
in our lives who inspired this book.

Jana Kolpen & Mary Tiegreen

Editor: Dervla Kelly
Designer: Mary Tiegreen
Production Manager: Kim Tyner

Library of Congress Cataloging-in-Publication Data

Kolpen, Jana Fayne.
  The circle of kindness : an Irish journey of the heart /
by Jana Kolpen and Mary Tiegreen.
      p. cm.
  ISBN-13: 978-1-58479-458-5
  ISBN-10: 1-58479-458-5
  1. Cookery, Irish--Fiction. 2. Gifts--Fiction. 3.
Ireland--Fiction. I. Tiegreen, Mary. II. Title.

PS3561.O4415C57 2006
813'.54--dc22   2006004634

Text copyright © 2006 by Jana Kolpen and Mary Tiegreen
Watercolor illustrations copyright © 2006 by Jana Kolpen
Photographs, scans, and electronic assemblages copyright
    © 2006 by Mary Tiegreen
Compilation copyright © 2006 by
    Stewart, Tabori & Chang

Published in 2006 by Stewart, Tabori & Chang
An imprint of Harry N. Abrams, Inc.

All rights reserved. No portion of this book may be
reproduced, stored in a retrieval system, or transmitted in
any form or by any means, mechanical, electronic,
photocopying, recording, or otherwise, without written
permission from the publisher.

The text of this book was composed in Bernhard Modern,
Powhatten, Poetica Chancery, and Girls are Weird.

Printed and bound in China
10 9 8 7 6 5 4 3 2 1

HNA ▨▨▨▨▨
harry n. abrams, inc.
a subsidiary of La Martinière Groupe
115 West 18th Street
New York, NY 10011
www.hnabooks.com